# HOW TO MAKE A BIRD

Meg McKinlay

illustrated by Matt Ottley

CANDLEWICK PRESS

To make a bird . . .

you will need a lot of very tiny bones.
They will be smaller than you might imagine,
some so tiny they are barely there.

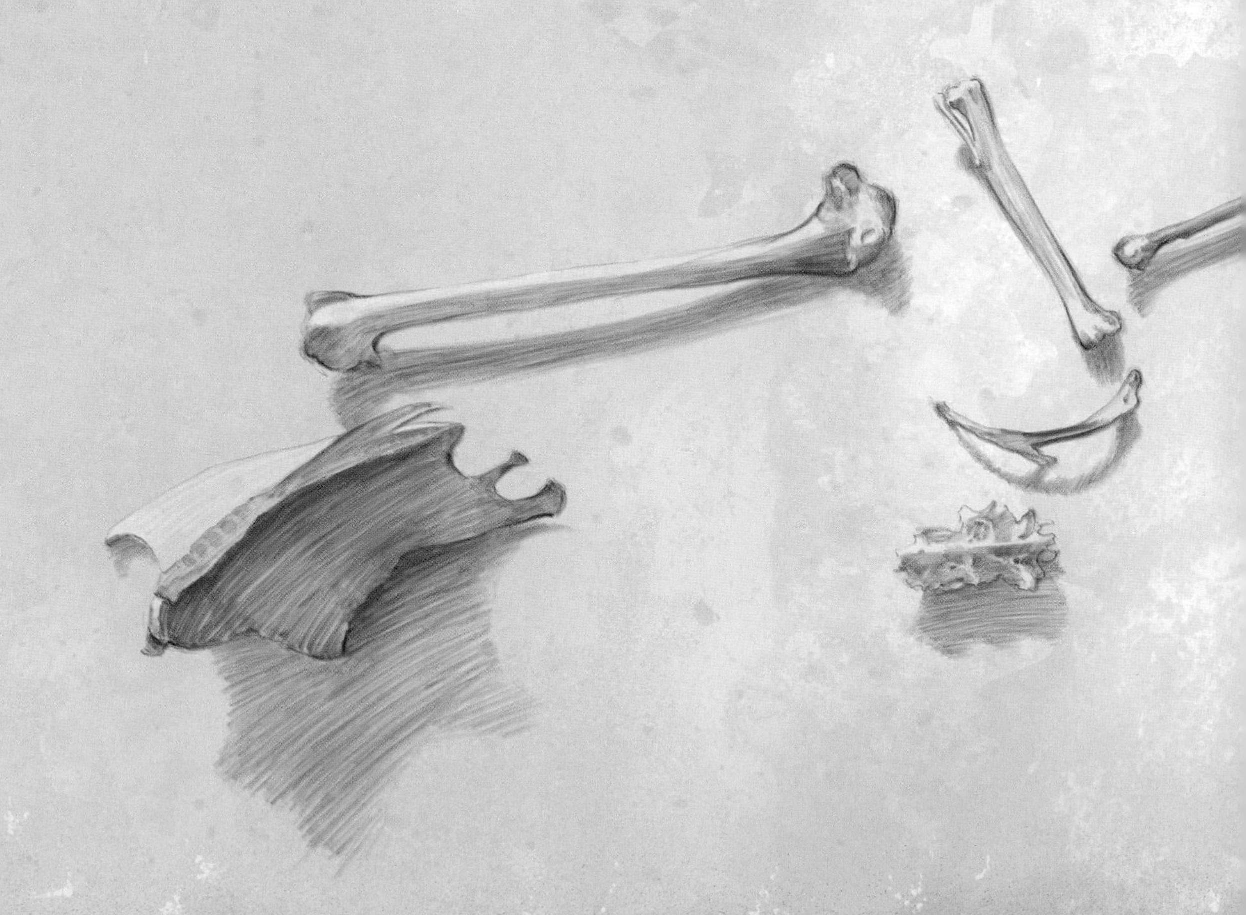

And they will be hollow,
these hundreds of bones—
so light

that when they rest in your palm,
you will hardly feel them.

These are what will float on air.

Take these bones
and arrange them into a bird shape.
Any bird shape will do—

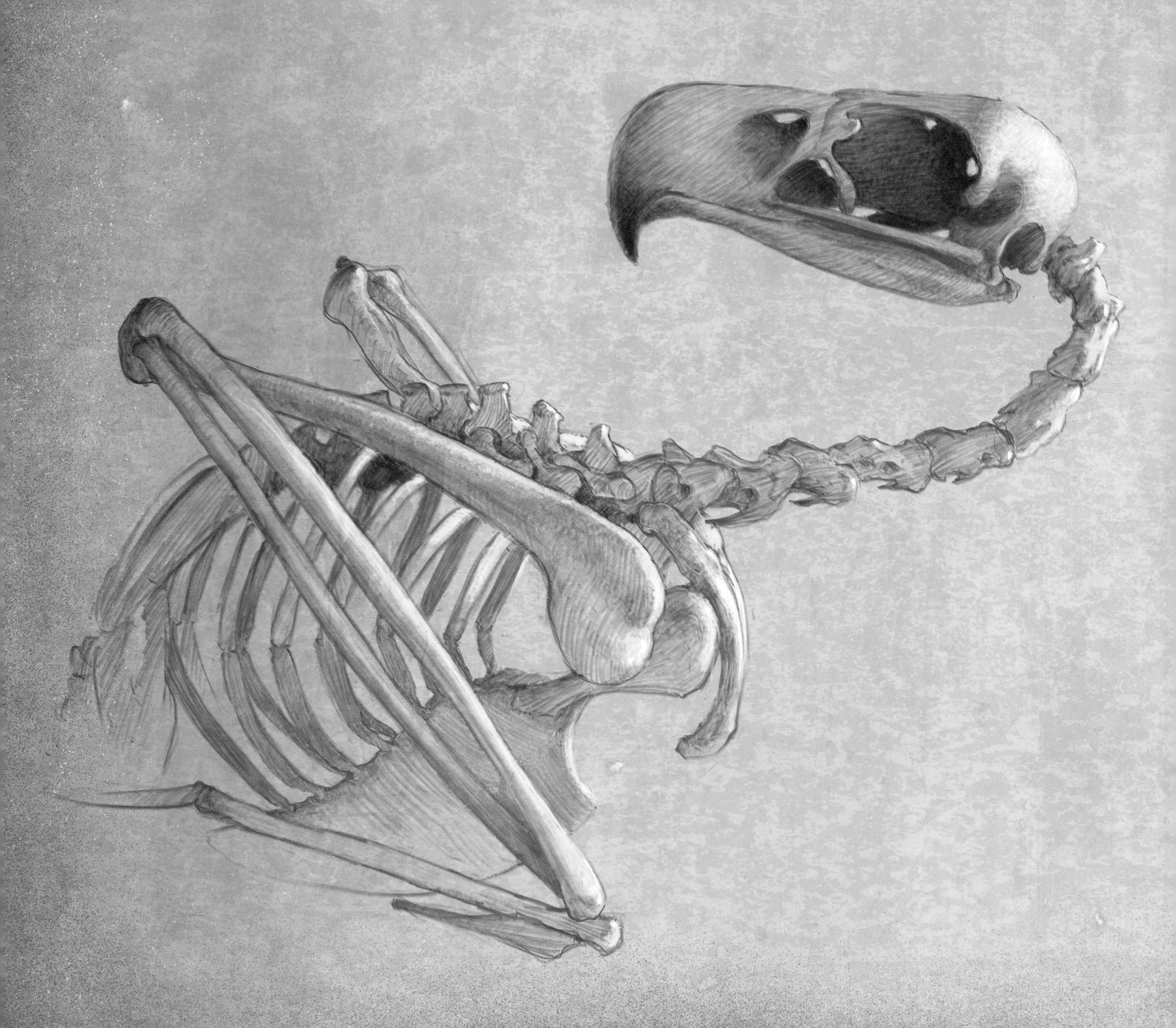

the proud arch of an eagle,

the soft curve of a sparrow.

Breathe deeply
and take your time.
The making of a bird
is not a thing
to be hurried.

Next you need feathers—
for warmth
and for flight.
Smooth these over the bones
of your bird shape;
press them firmly into place.

Save the longest feathers
for the wings and the tail;

these are what will lift
your bird into the air.

Now give your bird,
inside its brittle bones,
a heart that beats faster
than any human heart—

a sure, steady heart
to carry it across oceans
and continents,
all the way home
at the end of a long winter.

Then add the final touches,
the way an artist adds her last few brushstrokes,
her tiny signature.

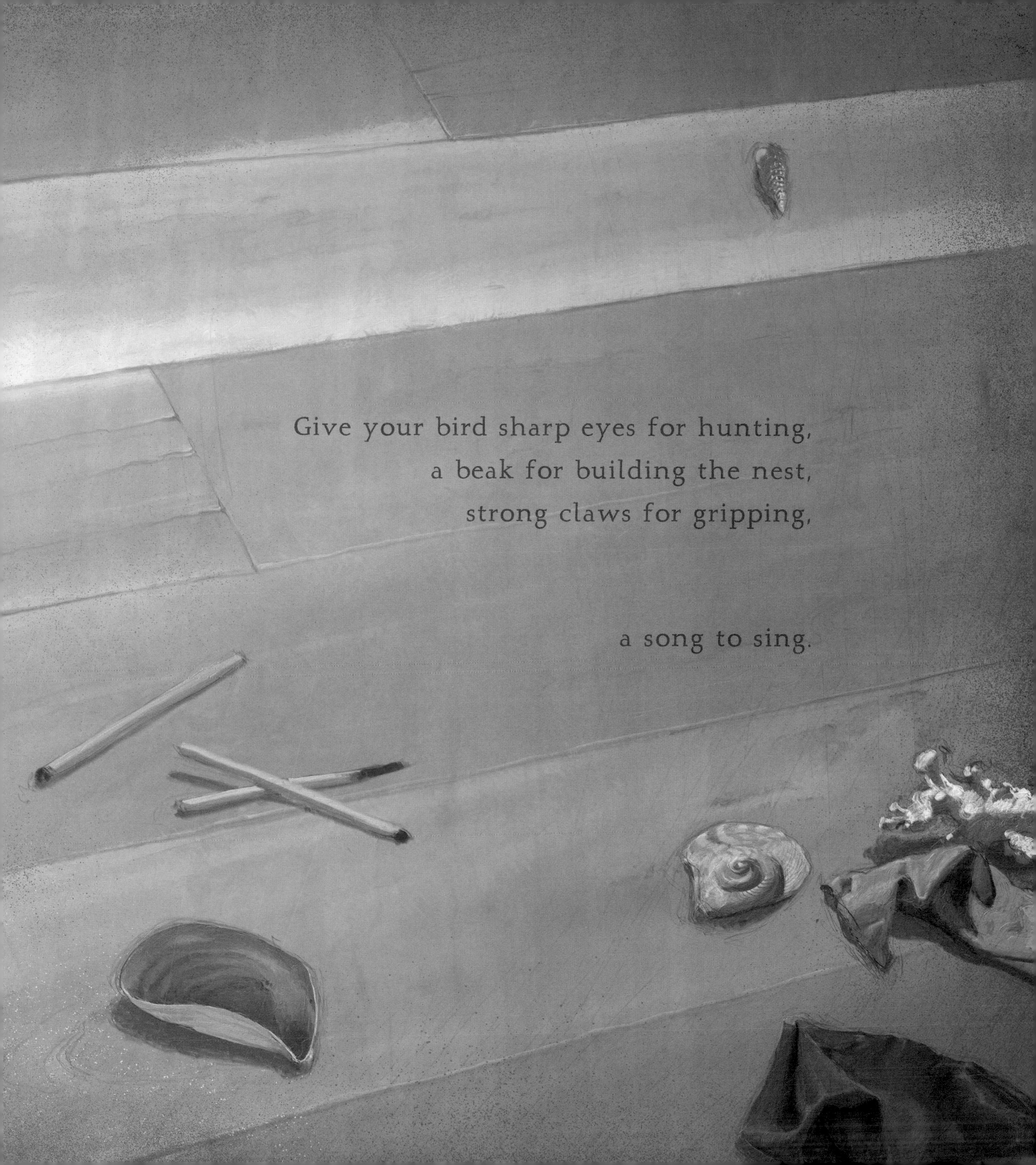

Give your bird sharp eyes for hunting,
a beak for building the nest,
strong claws for gripping,

a song to sing.

And when you have made your bird,
with its bones and its feathers
and its grasping claws,
you might sit back and sigh.

You might say to yourself,
*I have made this bird,*

*this silent, still, shape of a bird.*

But when you see it sitting,
cold as a statue, you will know
that there is more to a bird than
these things you have given it.

So you will gather it into your hands
and cast it gently upon the air.

Those wings you so carefully made
will stretch out just a little,
and your bird will tremble
as it fills, inside its tiny, racing heart,
with the dreams only a bird can dream . . .

of open sky and soaring flight.

And then your bird will catch your eye,
and you will know it is time to go
and open the window.

Open it.

Set your bird upon the sill and watch
while it stretches its wings
and looks around
with its clear, sharp eyes.

See it shiver
as it leans forward onto the air
and then takes off
in a strong, sudden movement,
soaring straight up . . .

away and away,
never once looking back,

until it is a disappearing speck
in a vast blue sky.

And feel your slowly beating heart fill
with a kind of sadness,
a kind of happiness.

For this is when you will know
that you have really made a bird.

To all the makers out there . . .
to everyone who has the
courage to breathe life
and let go

MM

For my friend Bomsan,
free as the sky

MO



*First US edition 2021
First published by Walker Books Australia 2020*

*Library of Congress Catalog Card Number pending
ISBN 978-1-5362-1526-7*

*LEO 25 24 23 22 21 20
10 9 8 7 6 5 4 3 2 1*

*Printed in Heshan, Guangdong, China*

*This book was typeset in Calligraphic Antique.
The illustrations were done in pigmented ink.*

*Candlewick Press
99 Dover Street
Somerville, Massachusetts 02144*

*www.candlewick.com*